The Old Man of Lochnagar

H.R.H. The Prince of Wales

The Old Man of Lochnagar

Illustrations by Sir Hugh Casson K.C.V.O.

PUFFIN BOOKS

Part One

Not all that long ago, when children were even smaller and people had especially hairy knees, there lived an old man of Lochnagar. He had made his house in a cave by the Loch of Lochnagar and it was a surprisingly comfortable cave. The door was made of deer skin and the doorknob consisted of a stag's antler which, when pressed, prodded a tame grouse and made it cry out "Go back, go back!" That way the old man succeeded in remaining totally alone for years and years and years.

One day he decided to see if he could climb up the cliff of Lochnagar. With much puffing and blowing he pulled himself up by his fingernails, but as he was nearing the top he lost his grip (in which he had his toothbrush and pyjamas) and he plunged down, down, down to the loch below. He hit it with an almighty splash, so big that everyone who was living at Balmoral in those days thought it was a huge rainstorm.

The old man was so big and fat after many years of living on grouse pâté and blaeberry pie that he sank deeper and deeper into the Loch. He rather enjoyed gliding down through the dark green water (you see, he could breathe underwater because he had amphibious nostrils and webbed eyebrows), and on the way down he passed hundreds of trout of different sizes. Some were enormous and were busy chasing the smaller ones, who could easily outmanoeuvre them because they were nimble and agile and didn't eat very much.

After an hour of sinking he came to the bottom with a dull thud. (It was a dull thud because most thuds aren't very interesting and anyway you can't hear much underwater.) He picked himself up – because there was no one else to do it for him – and looked around. There, sitting on a cushion of loch-weed, sat the Scottish freshwater variant of Neptune. He is called ''lagopus Scoticus'' in freshwater circles and always carries a double-handed bagpipe, with which he blows gaelic bubbles. These bubbles can knock people down underwater and that is the way lagopus Scoticus keeps people under control in his kingdom.

The old man went up and paid his respects to lagopus Scoticus. The only way they could talk underwater was by mouthing the words which appeared on the insides of bubbles as they floated up to the surface. You had to be quick, reading what the person was saying, otherwise they disappeared. A lot of mistakes have been made this way underwater and people are constantly accusing each other of being deaf or blind or not paying attention.

Lagopus Scoticus invited the old man to accompany him on a Loch-haggis shoot that day. So they climbed into a sea-rover and drove off across the loch bottom. They had Nagar maids as loaders and stood in weird butts waiting for the first covey of Loch-haggis to appear over the horizon. As it was a good year a lot of haggis were driven over the shooters. They are very difficult things to hit because they swim in short, sharp bursts and, owing to one leg being longer than the other two, they tend to revolve at the same time. However, the old man succeeded in getting twenty in one drive and altogether they got 100 thrace in the day. (Loch-haggis are counted in threes because the females have two husbands and lagopus Scoticus keepers don't know their two-times table.)

After the shoot the old man feasted on Loch-haggis and suffered terribly from wind afterwards. But it didn't stop him falling asleep by the side of the loch.

Part Two

When the old man woke up it was a glorious sunny day and the bees were buzzing busily amongst the heather so that they would be able to make lots of honey to keep hundreds of children sticky and full at tea-time. The old man had a slight hangover after all the Loch-haggis he had eaten and he sat holding his head in his hands. Then he held it in his feet and, finally, between his teeth, to see if it felt any better that way. He coughed loudly, blew his nose on a lily pad which he always carried in his pocket, rubbed his eyes and squinted at the sun which shone relentlessly down on him. It was then that he began to sneeze: he sneezed and sneezed and sneezed. "Ahhhhh-tishoooo! Ahhhhhhhhh-tishoooooooo!" Finally he sneezed so violently that the force directed into the ground acted like a rocket and shot him up, up into the air. He whizzed up so far that he landed on the top of Lochnagar and narrowly missed hitting his wrinkled bottom (because he was an old man, don't forget) on a sharp rock.

Once he had got over his surprise at being where he was the old man was delighted he had at last reached the summit of Lochnagar, because he had never managed it before. Nearby was a convenient stone cairn which some kind and thoughtful person had built just in case the old man felt like standing on it. He climbed up and looked at the view. It was while he was standing there admiring the view that a large golden eagle swooped from a great height and grabbed the old man by the shoulders.

The old man was by no means light, so the eagle had a very tough job getting his cargo airborne. There was much groaning and grunting, which was interesting scientifically because few people have ever heard an eagle grunt. (The secret to this was that this particular eagle was a pig-eagle – there are other sorts called fish-eagles.) Eventually the eagle took off and rose higher and higher into the blue sky. When they had reached a great height the old man looked down and saw Balmoral far below him, looking like a small toy. The eagle, too, looked down and, as he did so, the old man tickled him under the wingpits and, with an eagle-giggle, he dropped his burden. Down, down, down fell the old man, enjoying every second of it, because falling through the air can be great fun. Fortunately, he fell straight onto a trampoline that the children had been given for Christmas. His first bounce sent him up to 1,000 feet; his second to 500 feet; his third to 250 feet; until eventually, after many boing-boings, he came to a halt. In order to cool off and recover from the exhausting flight and dreadful bouncing, the old man climbed into the fountain and sat there with just his head showing.

Along came Mr Toad, who happened to have the tenancy of the fountain, and asked if he could help in any way. "Yes, please, if you would," said the old man, "I would like to get back to my cave as soon as possible." "Only too easy, my dear fellow," said Mr Toad. "Hang on to my foot and say after me: 'The Wind in the Willows, ker-bang, tiddly-splash'." He did so and at once there was a low rumbling sound followed by a swooshing noise and the old man found himself hurtling across the heather at terrific speed. He was back in his cave before he knew where he was and as Mr Toad disappeared back to the fountain with giant DOINGGGGG leaps the old man was lying on his comfy bed snoring his head off and occasionally putting it back on when he woke up to a really loud snore.

Part Three

When the old man woke up after several days asleep (because the air makes one *very* sleepy around Lochnagar), he pulled on his tartan knickerbockers and thought about breakfast. He made some heather porridge and squeezed the juice out of clover flowers onto his porridge to make it sweet. After all the activity of the previous days he felt extremely hungry and decided to have cooked breakfast as well. So he fried a ptarmigan's egg and some deer bacon.

After all this food he was really in no state to do anything, but he went first to the lavatory (always a good thing to do after breakfast), which he had built underneath two huge boulders near the cave. It was a splendid affair and he was rightly very proud of it. It had a finely carved stone door and a lock made of stag's horn. The seat was upholstered in leather, made from a stag's skin, and stuffed with finest down and feathers from several grouse. The actual mechanism of the 'loo was very cunning. The old man had found an antique pair of bagpipes and rigged them up so that when he pulled on a certain part of it, it not only flushed the lavatory, but played his favourite Scottish tune as well.

The old man read all sorts of books in his comfy 'loo. He got them from the friendly little people who inhabited the stone cairns near Lochnagar. They wrote fascinating stories and left them under a certain stone for the old man to collect. He had never actually been invited to their home, but they had told him a lot about it. Although the cairns look small from outside, in fact, if you could find the secret entrance, you would discover that a long flight of steps led down underground to a series of large rooms, corridors and halls. They had told him that they had cairngorm and amethyst chandeliers glittering in each room and that the floors were laid with the finest polished quartz (that white stone you find on the hillside). One day, they promised, he would see it all for himself, but this would only be possible when their research scientists had discovered the right formula for a potion which, when drunk, would shrink the old man to the size of the little people, who were called Gorms. (That is why people living in Scotland who don't have Gorms on their hills are called "gormless".)

After the old man had finished his morning toiletries he decided it was time he went on an expedition to Loch Muick. He hadn't been there for a long time and anyway he wanted a change of trout for his dinner and to get some blaeberries, which were particularly delicious over there. He climbed on a rock and cupped his hands to his mouth and gave a curious tuk-tuk-tukking call which echoed across the valleys. Very soon it was answered by a similar sound followed by a gentle swishing which grew

louder and louder. Soon there was a noise of wings beating and twelve
huge cock capercaillie came up the valley in perfect formation and settled
beside the old man. He gave each one of them a pat and a daddy-long-legs
to eat (because they liked daddy-long-legs in the same way that horses
like sugar). The old man went to his cave and harnessed a special caper
carriage to the twelve birds – six on one side and six on the other – then

he climbed into his seat and called to them to take off. They were immensely powerful birds and soon the carriage was soaring higher and higher as the caper beat their wings with effortless ease. The only problem to face was where to land at Loch Muick because of the steep sides and masses of trees. But the old man had solved this by putting floats on his carriage and making the caper fly low over the loch so that he sank onto the water like a flying boat and ended up on the beach. He gave the caper a thank-you pat and more of the sugared daddy-long-legs before setting off to catch some trout.

He didn't do this with a rod. Instead he gave a strange screech and two beautiful ospreys swooped down from the towering crags above the loch. Ospreys are rather like eagles, only smaller and somewhat greyer. They live on fish and catch them by diving onto them from a great height and picking them up in their talons. The old man had trained these two to fish for him and one was called Skean and the other Dhu. The old man gave them their instructions and they rose up far above the loch to look for some trout. When they spied some they plummeted down together and disappeared with two great splashes, to reappear a second later clutching two fine trout. The old man decided to cook his dinner there and then and they all sat round a roaring fire – the old man, the caper and the ospreys – eating fish and blaeberries, telling one another stories of the old days and singing strange gaelic songs, while the moon rose higher and higher above the gently rustling pine trees.

Part Four

By the time the old man, the ospreys and the caper had finished gossiping and singing, it was very late at night and the owl that lives at Loch Muick was flitting through the trees telling them they ought to be home and asleep. Now it was a long time since the old man had tried to fly back to Lochnagar in the dark but, as the moon was full and the twelve caper seemed quite happy to try it, he climbed into his carriage, said goodbye to the ospreys (who by now were completely drunk from eating too many blaeberries and were in an unfit state to fly), and took off across the loch. The glimmering surface of the water dropped away beneath as they climbed to the star-filled sky, but suddenly the caper had to make a steep bank to port in order to avoid flying straight into the side of the loch. The old man wasn't really paying attention because he was so sleepy; in fact he was dozing and so he very nearly fell out as they went round the corner. He woke up with a start and kept an eye out after that.

They had a fairly exciting flight back to Lochnagar, particularly when they were flying over the top of a high peak and the bottom of the carriage

struck a rock. The old man had a nasty fright and called to the caper to look out for any further obstructions, but they soon landed safely near the cave and the old man unhitched the caper and watched them flap off silently into the darkness, back to the forest they had come from. The old man only had a few hours' sleep before it was time to get up again. When he did get up he felt a bit ill because he had eaten too many blaeberries and his mouth and teeth were bright purple from all the juice. He pottered off to his washbasin, which he had made out of a piece of granite, and brushed his teeth as hard as he could with toothpaste made from bog myrtle and wild mint. He had a terrible weakness for this toothpaste and was always cleaning his teeth so that he could have this delicious stuff to eat.

While he was sitting having his breakfast a grouse with a wicked look in its eye flew into the cave and settled on the table. In its beak it was carrying a message, which it conveniently dropped into the scrambled eggs. The old man opened the message, wondering what it could be and, upon reading it, discovered it was an invitation at long last from the little Gorm people to visit their cairn home. The message was wrapped round a small bottle of green liquid and the instructions on it said it was to be taken outside the entrance to the cairn. But the old man didn't think there was any need to wait till then because it smelt rather good and he never bothered about instructions on bottles. In this case it was an unwise thing to do because before he had gone a few steps from the cave he began to shrink and grow smaller and smaller. Very soon his shoes flopped around his tiny feet and his clothes completely enveloped him in

a smothering heap. With great difficulty he clambered out through a hole in his breast pocket and found that he had to make his way through giant clumps of heather and gigantic boulders. It was like fighting your way through an impenetrable jungle and very soon he grew boiling hot and thought he would never make the cairn. On the way he passed spiders not much smaller than himself and had to be very careful not to walk into one of their high-tensile webs, which they spin to catch unwary flies.

Eventually, he arrived, puffing and perspiring, at the door to the cairn, where he found a little group of Gorms doubled up with helpless laughter at the sight of the shrunken old man hacking his way through the heather. They were very nearly sick, they laughed so much, but the old man was not amused in the slightest. He scowled at them and wiped a bead of perspiration off the end of his nose. At length the little people recovered and invited the old man to come in. Everything seemed enormous now that he was so small, and he very nearly slipped and fell flat on his back when he took one step on the highly polished floor. The Gorms burst out laughing again, but realized that they were being rude and stopped.

In front of the old man stretched a long flight of steps leading down towards a dazzling light at the bottom. On either side of the steps great cairngorms shone with a strange golden light, and above them hung the magnificent heads of stag beetles. When they came to the bottom of the steps the old man found himself in a vast hall with a shining wooden floor and the fabulous cairngorm and amethyst chandeliers he had heard

so much about. At the far end of the room sat the king of the Gorms on a
huge throne made from a single amethyst and studded with garnets.

Part Five

To the old man it was a dazzling sight and for a moment he thought that the king had at least six legs and six heads, such was the reflecting quality of the amethyst. That filled him with awe and he approached the throne with immense care, not quite knowing what to do next. A little man, who looked very important, whispered in his ear and the old man bowed three times as he approached. On the third bow his feet slipped from under him and he slid on his bottom on the slippery floor right up to the foot of the throne. The little Gorms had a laughing disease, because they all broke into fits of helpless giggles as the old man floundered about on the floor with his legs waving in the air, rather as a fly does on the window sill when it's exhausted. When he got up he shook hands with the king, who had risen from his throne and invited him to have a glass of rowan wine in his drawing-room. The old man noticed that the king had very thick rubber soles to his shoes and that fastened to his bottom there was a peculiar rubber mat. He had to wear

this to prevent him slipping off this throne all the time, and anyway several of his ancestors had either died from a chilled bottom or were crippled for life by sliding off their thrones in the middle of audiences. Such Gorm disasters encouraged the development of these bottom pads.

Having sipped some rowan wine with the king and queen, who was a charming person and had lots of tiny Gorms running about her, they went off on a tour of the underground kingdom. They passed rows of workshops where little people were busy pouring molten copper into moulds. At night they would set out and put the leaves onto the branches of copper beech trees so that they would always be bright and shining all summer. In another room more Gorms were stirring a huge cauldron of purple liquid which smelt like heather honey. In the early mornings, long before anyone awoke, little Gorm heathercraft could be seen flying to and fro over the hills spraying out the purple liquid. If they didn't do that, the heather wouldn't be as beautiful and purple as it is.

A bit farther on they came to a huge hall where large numbers of women Gorms were milking hind stag beetles. Unfortunately, stag beetles are incredibly ticklish, so the noise during milking was almost indescribable. The milkmaids found it difficult to do their job because the beetles kept shaking up and down so much with hysterics. The old man was given a drink of beetle milk by the head milkmaid, which he pronounced excellent, but the effects were somewhat disturbing. The milk diluted the special shrinking mixture and the old man started to grow bigger much sooner than the Gorms had anticipated. With great difficulty they rushed him through the slippery passages and halls and *just* managed to heave and squeeze him out through the door in the cairn. The old man was exhausted and rather bruised after being squeezed like toothpaste through a small hole and he tottered slowly back to his cave, where he eased himself onto the bed and fell into a long, delicious sleep.

Part Six

One winter, over eighty years ago, the old man of Lochnagar decided that it was high time he travelled down to London to see the sights of the city that he had heard stories about so often. You may well wonder how he knew of the existence of London when he had spent all his life in a cave in the hills. The answer is quite simple really. You remember how he was given a special shrinking-mixture to drink by the Gorms so that he could go into their cairns? Well, he sometimes used this mixture so that he could creep up unseen on people having picnics in the heather and listen to their conversation. In between mouthfuls of delicious food, these picnickers would constantly talk about what was going on in London – what was happening in the theatres or at the opera, or who had given a better party than Mrs So & So. If the truth be known, in fact, the old man was far more interested in watching the food than listening to the conversation. One day he was rewarded beyond all expectation when a whole ginger biscuit landed with a thud beside him. Now don't forget, the old man had made himself very small, so the ginger biscuit was almost exactly the same size as him and it is no joke to have

such an enormous thing narrowly miss you like that. Eventually, he managed to break bits off it by jumping up and down in the middle with his hobnail boots.

Anyway, it was at the beginning of December, when everything was lying silent under a thick blanket of soft snow, and only the criss-cross tracks in the whiteness indicated that there was anything alive in the hills, that the old man decided it was a good time to make the expedition south. He hitched his two best stags to his long-distance sledge and set off for Ballater, where he knew that there was a train which went to London by devious routes. Now, as it was over eighty years ago, the trains were not as fast as they are now and they did not have beds in them either, but there was masses to eat and he didn't mind sitting for hours because the whole thing was a great treat and there was some beautiful scenery to look at on the way.

The train heaved its way out of Ballater station in a great cloud of steam and smoke, which eventually enveloped all the people standing on the platform. The old man was hanging out of the windows as they left and, as the smoke cleared, he saw one gentleman wearing a huge top hat walk straight into the wall of the ticket office. He was obviously short-sighted, or had been disorientated by the smoke, because he staggered about for some minutes and finally fell onto a passing luggage trolley, which disappeared through a side door. ''Poor chap!'' thought the old man.

No sooner had they reached Aboyne than everything came to a grinding halt. Bits of luggage and hat boxes flew off the luggage rack and fell on top of people in the carriages. ''What the deuce!'' exclaimed a red-faced, bewhiskered gentleman in a fur-lined kilt (who sat opposite the old man), as he was showered with a multitude of personal belongings. ''What the deuce, indeed!'' echoed a formidable lady in the corner of the carriage. She presented an extraordinary picture, being entirely swathed in tartan from head to foot and with a hat that was vast and bore a distinct resemblance to a stuffed grouse – complete with feet! On the end of her nose, precariously balanced, sat a pair of pince-nez and through them peered a set of beady blue eyes which had, up till then, been focused upon a curious bundle of knitting in her lap. The cause of the halt had turned out to be a herd of cows which had strayed onto the line, but they were soon cleared off and the train was again lurching its way southward. All the way to Aberdeen the Dee could be seen almost completely frozen over and the trees were bent down with piles of snow.

When the train reached Aberdeen, disaster struck. Heavy falls of snow had blocked the track on the line to London, and the station-master announced that it would take several days to clear it. The formidable lady with the huge hat was positively clucking with indignation and, as the old man reluctantly boarded a return train to Ballater, he caught sight of her on the platform, angrily prodding the station-master with her umbrella.

So it was that the old man failed to reach London. Secretly he was rather pleased, for he hated leaving his cave and his friends who lived in the hills around him. The stories he had heard from the picnickers were all he needed to know about London. He couldn't think of anywhere more special to be, than to be living at the foot of Lochnagar.

THE END